D0404852

CHRISTMAS IN JULY

BEARPAW RIDGE FIREFIGHTERS NOVELLA

OPHELIA SEXTON

Published by Philtata Press, LLC
Text copyright 2019 by Ophelia Sexton. All rights reserved.
Cover art by Jacqueline Sweet

This ebook is licensed for your personal enjoyment only. This ebook may not be resold or given away to other people. If you would like to share this book with another person, please purchase an additional copy for each recipient. If you're reading this book and did not purchase it, or it was not purchased for your use only, then please return to your favorite ebook retailer and purchase your own copy. Thank you for respecting the hard work of this author.

AUTHOR'S NOTE

This story was born last autumn, when my home state of California was ravaged by immensely destructive wildfires for the second year in a row. Although my own town escaped lightly, with just a few grass fires, two cities to the north of me, Santa Rosa and Paradise, suffered devastating losses.

In both cases, when CalFire and local fire departments were overwhelmed and exhausted by the gargantuan scale of these wildfires, other firefighters came to their aid from all over the United States, western Canada, Mexico, and even Australia.

Without their help, even more homes and lives would have been lost in those dark days, when the air was so thick with smoke that everyone living within hundreds of miles of the fires had to wear masks just to leave their homes and run errands or go to work.

The second impetus for this story arrived last December, in the form of an unexpected Christmas gift sent by one of my Australian Facebook friends, Sam Wilson. It was an Australian firefighters charity calendar, very similar in concept to the one I described in *Smoke*. It currently adorns the wall of my home office and serves as a source of constant inspiration.

Thank you, Sam! (And yes, as promised, I did name the hero of this story after you...)

1

TENT CITY

"**I** don't think we made enough sandwiches. Or brought enough coffee," Annabeth Jones Swanson said, frowning, as her assistant Hannah Swanson maneuvered Cinnamon + Sugar's big tan-and-pink catering van into the Lemhi County Fairgrounds' parking lot.

Hannah's eyes widened as she saw that an entire city had sprouted in the lot practically overnight.

Orderly rows of tents, interspersed with long trailers that served as showers and first aid stations, faced rank upon rank of parked fire engines. Hannah spotted license plates from twenty US states, as well as the Canadian provinces of British Columbia and Alberta.

Above the fairgrounds, the sun burned orange in a dull brown sky. The air smelled of smoke, and the sharp ridges and peaks of the mountains on either side of the valley had disappeared behind a thick, choking haze.

After one of the driest Junes on record, Bearpaw Ridge and its neighboring communities now lay in the path of a huge and destructive firestorm. Firefighters from all over North America had converged here in an effort to save the town.

This wasn't the first time that fire had visited the vast national forests and BLM lands that surrounded Bearpaw Ridge. Wildfires were part of the natural ecology of the western ranges... though rarely with this breadth and intensity.

And whenever the town's all-volunteer fire department was called into action, Hannah and her boss Annabeth leaped into action to support the firefighters with hot coffee, cold drinks, hearty soups and sandwiches, and of course, Annabeth's famous pastries.

"I think we're going to be making a few more runs out here today," Hannah agreed, as she slowly drove past a row of parked fire engines.

She passed a ladder truck from the Alameda County Fire Department in California, then a tanker from Nashville, Tennessee, before Annabeth pointed excitedly at a group of grimy, tired-looking men and women dressed in firefighter gear. "There! I see Dane and the others!"

Hannah pulled up and parked as Annabeth scrambled out of the van.

One of the firefighters, tall and broad-shouldered in his heavy coat and turnouts, strode forward to meet them. His helmet was labeled "Chief."

He caught Annabeth up in his arms, and gave her a hearty kiss. Her wedding ring gleamed in the strange orange sunlight as she wound her arms around the fire chief's neck and enthusiastically returned the kiss.

"Hiya Dane!" Hannah greeted her cousin when he had released Annabeth from his embrace.

She looked past him and saw her other friends and relatives from the all-volunteer Bearpaw Ridge Fire Department. She waved at her cousins Mark, Tyler, and Ash, and her friend, Michael Jacobsen.

All of them looked tired and dirty from long hours spent in hard labor.

Her older sister Kayla, her face smeared with soot and dust under her helmet, walked over to give Hannah a hug.

"Hannah-banana, please tell me you brought some Diet Cokes," she begged, using Hannah's childhood nickname.

"A whole cooler full," Hannah assured her.

She looked around the group, trying to decide what to unload first from the bounty in the back of the van, and saw that the Bearpaw Ridge firefighters had been joined by a group of strangers.

Kayla saw her looking and grinned. "We made some new friends today. A group of firefighters came all the way from Queensland, Australia to help out! They said they have a mutual aid agreement with our state."

She waved at a tall man who was chatting with Mark. "Hey, Sam, do you want to meet my little sister Hannah?" she called.

The tall man's face brightened and he smiled broadly as he came over.

As he neared them, Hannah saw that he was about her age, with close-cropped, sun-streaked light brown hair, an attractively stubbled face, and bright blue eyes. He had shed his coat and wore a red t-shirt printed with "Queensland Fire and Rescue Services" stretched over his broad-shoulders and heavily muscled chest.

"G'day!" he greeted her with a wide smile. "I heard a rumor that you might be bringing us tea."

"Sure, we've got iced t—" Hannah began.

"He doesn't mean tea-the-beverage, he means supper," Kayla interrupted.

"Well, we've got that, too," Hannah assured him.

"Right-o," Sam replied, extending his hand. "I'm Sam Wilson. How're ya going?"

"Hannah Swanson." She shook his big, callused hand and felt a jolt like an electric shock travel up her arm.

His blue eyes widened, as if he'd just felt the same shock.

Then the breeze shifted, carrying his scent to her despite the choking pall of smoke.

He's a bear shifter, just like me!

2

THE SHIFTER FROM DOWN UNDER

They stared at each other in wordless recognition, their hands still clasped.

After a few moments, Kayla cleared her throat.

"Hannah, do you need some help unloading the van?" she asked pointedly, though her hazel eyes sparkled with mischief.

"Uh," Hannah said. She felt dazed. *Van? What van?*

Sam was still holding her hand, and she liked the feeling of his strong fingers around hers.

"I'll help," he volunteered, and released her.

Hannah immediately regretted the loss of contact, but forced herself to focus on the reason she and Annabeth had come here. "Thanks!"

She opened the van's back doors, which were painted with Cinnamon + Sugar's trademark pink curlicue font logo, and began pulling out big trays of sandwiches covered with plastic wrap.

She handed the first two trays to Sam, and saw Annabeth approaching, tailed by a group of firefighters.

For the next few minutes, Annabeth and Hannah handed off trays of sandwiches, fruit, cookies, and portable coolers filled with chilled bottles of water and cans of soda to eager hands.

The weary firefighters placed them on nearby picnic tables, then began helping themselves to the bounty.

The last items to come out of the van were the huge airpots of coffee.

"Let me give you a hand with those," said a pleasantly deep voice from behind her, flavored with an Aussie accent.

Hannah's shifter strength meant that she didn't really need any help...but it was nice of Sam to offer. "Thanks. That's really sweet of you."

He smiled at her, and she felt a rush of warmth kindle in her chest. "No worries," he said, cheerfully. "It's the least I can do in return for all this tucker."

As he stepped close to take the bulky airpot from her arms, he murmured, "You smell really good. Like cinnamon and vanilla."

Her heart began pounding at his proximity. "Uh, thank you?"

She fought the temptation to go up tiptoes, and bury her nose in the curve where his neck met his shoulder, and chase his intriguing masculine scent underneath the layers of smoke and sweat.

"I feel like I've been smelling nothing but smoke all day," he added, his tone apologetic.

Hannah kept sneaking glances at him as she set up the coffee station and opened the coolers filled with drinks.

Then, things got busy as she and Annabeth handed out food and drinks to the hungry, weary firefighters crowding around them.

Over the next few minutes, she overheard that things were very challenging on the fire lines, due to the gusty winds driving the fire in unpredictable directions.

The Bearpaw Ridge firefighters and their Australian counterparts had spent most of the day clearing brush and digging firebreaks in an attempt to keep the advancing flames from devouring homes on the town's far-flung fringes.

When only crumbs remained on the trays, most of the firefighters began heading towards the bathroom trailers to grab hot showers before collapsing on their cots.

At dawn, the hard, dirty, dangerous work would begin anew.

Sam approached as Hannah and Annabeth were gathering up the trays.

He cast a sideways glance at Dane, who was bending to lift one of the large coolers, then asked in a low voice. "So, me and my mates were wondering if you were planning to return tomorrow?"

Hannah smiled at him. "We'll be coming here every day until the fires are under control."

The young Australian firefighter brightened. "Can we trade mobile numbers? I was hoping that you might text me when you're headed out this way again?"

A thrill ran through Hannah at his words. He was so nice...and so good-looking, even under a layer of sooty stubble.

"Ask her if she'll bring more of those apple turnovers!" shouted one of the other Aussies.

Annabeth dimpled and tucked a stray lock of her strawberry-blonde hair under her turquoise-colored chef's cap. "Absolutely. I'll make a double batch for tomorrow. Anything else I can bring you?"

The air was immediately filled with shouts and suggestions. Annabeth's peanut butter cookies were requested by multiple voices, as were the roast beef sandwiches, made with grass-fed beef from the Swanson family's Grizzly Creek Ranch.

Hannah just finished entering her number in Sam's cellphone when he handed her phone back with a wicked grin. "I've got a request: ask your boss to bring you back here tomorrow."

Hannah couldn't help smiling back. She'd sworn off dating after some major disappointments, but Sam was yummy-looking. And sweet.

"Only if you promise you'll be here," she told him, smiling.

3

THUNDERSTRUCK

He's the one, Sam Wilson's bear rumbled silently. *She's meant to be ours.*

Feeling thunderstruck, he watched the tan-and-pink bakery van drive away in a cloud of dust.

He'd grown up on his family's farm on the outskirts of a small town in the Darling Downs area of Queensland. There'd been many times when he felt like a freak because the Wilsons were the only shifters in the area.

When he had joined Queensland Fire and Emergency Services, he'd never dreamed that he'd get the opportunity to travel all the way to America, much less to a place where shifters seemed to outnumber the Ordinaries.

Despite the long hours of hard labor so far, Sam had been relishing the experience of working side-by-side with Dane

Swanson and his crew. For the first time in his life, he didn't have to watch his every move for fear of betraying his shifter strength and enhanced senses.

Since he'd arrived a couple of days ago, Sam had been working shoulder-to-shoulder with bear shifters, wolf shifters, and several different kinds of cat shifters—cougar, jaguar, lynx, and something else that he couldn't identify.

"So, it looks like you two really hit it off," Kayla Swanson said with a sunny smile as she came to stand next to him.

Sam felt his face heat. "She isn't involved with anyone, is she?" *Please say no...*

To his relief, Kayla shook her head. "Nope. All she does is work at Annabeth's bakery and go home. I keep telling her that she needs to get out there and live a little."

"She's single? Beauty!" breathed Sam. It was the best news he'd heard all day.

He weighed his mobile phone in his hand. *She gave me her number. That means she's interested in getting to know me, right?*

Before coming here, he'd never met any other bear shifters outside of his family. And especially not any female bear shifters.

If the Swanson girls were any indication, he'd been missing out. Kayla was attractive in a tomboyish way, but Hannah was downright luscious, with curves that made him ache to pull her in close and run his hands all over her. Her mouth looked just as soft and curving as the rest of her, and he just knew that kissing her would feel amazing…hot and sweet and wet.

He swallowed hard at the vivid fantasy, and felt his cock spring to throbbing life despite his aching muscles and bone-deep tiredness. *Thank God for these super-thick bunker pants, or I'd definitely be embarrassing myself right about now!*

"Awesome," said Kayla, sounding satisfied. "I'll put in a good word for you." She scrutinized him with a crooked grin. "You wouldn't happen to have any older—and single—brothers, would you?"

Sam shook his head. "Sorry, mate." '

"Aw, just my luck." Kayla shook her head ruefully, and marched off in the direction of the women's shower trailer.

Later, after he'd had a chance to wash off a day's worth of sweat and soot, he prepared to bunk down in the tent he shared with three other mates from QFES.

He opened a paperback thriller, but found that he couldn't stop thinking about Hannah Swanson, with her warm hazel eyes and her intoxicating perfume of cinnamon, vanilla, sugar, and sweet female musk. He found himself looking at his mobile, and debating whether he'd be coming on too strong if he texted her so soon.

In the end, he couldn't help himself. He put his book aside, sat up on his cot, and felt his heart pounding as he began typing.

Oi, H. Can't wait to see you tomorrow.

He frowned down at his phone, thinking that he sounded like a right galah, when his phone buzzed with Hannah's reply.

Looking forward to seeing you, too.

Sam breathed a sigh of relief, especially when he saw the cute budgie emoji appended to the end of her message. It was waving a miniature Australian flag.

Can you bring more of those choc chip biccies in the arvo?

Her reply came almost instantly. **Biccies? You mean cookies? What's an arvo? I'm not sure I have one of those.**

Sam chuckled, which earned him inquisitive looks from his mates.

Arvo = afternoon, he typed.

Right. I'll see you in tomorrow arvo, then, she replied, and appended a smiley face emoji. **Stay safe out there.**

"Hey, Sammo, you textin' that pretty Yank baker?" asked Ian from his cot. He'd just finished a Skype chat with his fiancée, and he tucked away his tablet with a sigh.

Sam grinned.

Ian whistled approvingly. "Good on ya!"

4
_____

NOT QUITE A DAMSEL IN DISTRESS

Hannah couldn't deny that she had butterflies in her stomach when she and Annabeth returned to the fairgrounds the next afternoon.

She'd gotten up even earlier than usual this morning, so that she could take some time with her hair instead of just putting it in her usual ponytail. She had even put on a bit of makeup in hopes of seeing Sam again.

But when the bakery's delivery van parked in the big lot near the Bearpaw Ridge FD's tents, she didn't see anyone she knew— either the volunteer firefighters from Bearpaw Ridge, or the Australian contingent.

Annabeth saw her peering around, and smiled reassuringly. "Dane just texted me. They're running a little late just trying to finish the firebreak in their section. They'll be here shortly... and they're giving the Aussie group a ride back down the ridge."

"Good," said Kayla, trying to keep from showing how nervous she felt about seeing Sam again.

She'd never reacted to any of her dates as strongly as she'd reacted to him yesterday. She hadn't been able to stop thinking about him. In fact, last night she'd spent hours re-running everything they'd said to each other when she should have been sleeping.

It felt...nice.

Nerve wracking as hell, but nice. Exciting.

The butterflies in her stomach only intensified as she helped Annabeth unload the van.

In anticipation of feeding two groups of hungry firefighters just off the line after a twelve-hour shift of intense physical labor, Hannah and Annabeth had brought twice as much food today, including extra batches of apple turnovers and chocolate chip cookies.

She was on her hands and knees in the back of the van, retrieving the last of a set of big rectangular metal pans, when she heard the sounds of several fire engines pulling up nearby and parking.

She heard the firm tread of approaching steps. Her heart began beating fast, and she felt dizzy with anticipation.

You've got to calm down, she told herself. *Or he's going to think you're some kind of psycho.*

"Well, if it isn't the big, sweet ass of my favorite little baker chick," drawled a familiar—and unwelcome—man's voice behind her. "Save a cookie for me?"

All of her excitement soured in an instant.

Hannah finished pulling the large pan of lasagna out of the van, straightened up, and slowly turned around.

Yep, it's Jake Lesours, all right. The smoky air had masked his scent, but his snotty tone hadn't changed a bit in the six months since she'd last seen him. They'd met through ShiftMatch, but within a half-hour of meeting him for first-date coffee, she had known that she had zero interest in a second date.

Which had been disappointing as hell, because his profile and his photo had both looked perfect.

Wearing a sweat-stained red Ourseville FD t-shirt and turn-outs, he looked a far cry from the neat and polished shifter of their first date. A day's worth of uneven stubble covered his cheeks and throat, and his turnouts were covered with dirt and soot.

The irony was that he actually looked more attractive now than he had when she first met him.

"Wow, look at you, trying to be all sexy," he observed with a smirk, eyeing her up and down.

Just like the first time she'd met him, he was offering her insults disguised as compliments, designed to throw her off-balance and undermine her self-confidence.

What a jerk.

Luckily, Hannah's self-confidence was pretty solid, especially when it came to guys that she had zero interest in... like Jake.

His gaze lingered on her waist-length dark brown hair. She had left it down today, held out of her face with a wide headband in a pretty tropical print.

Hannah rolled her eyes at his lame attempt at negging. "Thanks for confirming that I made the right decision to block you on ShiftMatch."

Then she turned her back on him.

"Yeah, about that—" he began.

She made a chopping gesture to indicate the conversation was over, picked up the pan, and turned to walk away.

Jake grabbed her arm. "Don't you walk away from me," he snarled. "I wasn't finished talking to you."

"But I'm done with this conversation," Hannah shot back. She tried and failed to break his grip. "Let go of me, Jake."

"What the hell's your problem, Hannah?" His fingers tightened with bruising force. "I was just trying to be nice, but thanks for reminding me that you're ugly and a bitch."

Nice? This was his version of nice?

"And thanks for reminding me that you're an asshole. Get your hands off me!"

"Oh, stop acting like a fucking drama queen," Jake ordered, his face twisting in rage. "I heard you can't get a date, so what's your problem?"

There was a blur of motion in Hannah's peripheral vision, then a sharp crack and popping noise.

The painful grip on her arm vanished, and her nose was suddenly filled with the familiar—and very welcome—scent of another bear shifter.

"She doesn't fancy wankers like you," Sam Wilson growled. "Especially ones who can't take 'no' for an answer. Piss off."

"You broke my wrist!" Jake was sprawled on the ground. "I'm going to fucking call the cops!"

Sam smiled pleasantly down at him. "And do what, mate? Explain how you were assaulting Hannah here?"

And if it came down to her word against Jake's, well, Hannah knew everyone on the small Bearpaw Ridge police force. And it appeared that there had been several witnesses to the incident, if her cousins' glowers in Jake's direction were anything to go by.

"Assault? I was just trying to apologize!" Jake protested. "It's not my fault that she can't take a—"

"That's funny," Sam interrupted. "Because you looked to me like you were about to slug her one. And I've never had someone to tell me to get my hands off them while I was apologizing."

He leaned over Jake, and his smile vanished. In a hard voice, he repeated, "Piss off."

Jake opened his mouth, then his eyes widened as Dane Swanson came up and surveyed the scene coolly.

"Get your wrist treated at the first-aid station and go home, Jake," he said, his tone even but underlaid with steel. "I don't want to see you around here again."

The rest of the Bearpaw Ridge contingent were close on Dane's heels.

All of the firefighters on duty today were shifters, mostly bear and wolf, with a couple of sabertooth cat shifters from the area's brand-new new Cougar Lake Pride. None of them looked very friendly at the moment as they stared down at the injured Jake.

Cradling his right arm against his body, Jake scrambled to his feet, glared at all of them, then stomped off without saying anything else.

Sam laid a big, protective hand on her shoulder. "You all right?"

The welcome heat of his touch soaked through her t-shirt and into her skin.

She realized she was swaying, leaning into him, and unobtrusively tried to pull back a little.

Her bear rose up in protest, making her skin prickle as if she were about shapeshift. It wanted Hannah to step closer and press herself against the tall, solidly-built Aussie. It wanted her to sink into his embrace.

"Thank you, Sam." Hannah's voice shook, but with pure need now instead of her rapidly-dissipating anger.

She looked around at the gathered firefighters and caught Kayla's eye.

Her sister's gaze was focused on Sam's hand, still resting on Hannah's shoulder. She grinned at Hannah and gave her a covert thumbs-up signal.

Hannah felt her cheeks heat, but couldn't stop the smile that bubbled up from inside her.

She was intensely aware that Sam hadn't removed his hand from her shoulder. And she didn't want him to.

She looked around the loose circle of her assembled relatives and friends.

"Talk about showing up in the nick of time!" she said to them, trying to keep her tone light. "I thought Jake was going to mug me for this lasagna! I'm glad I'd already unloaded the cookies and turnovers, or we would have been in real trouble!"

A ripple of laughter moved through the group. Then, with the exception of Sam, and Dane, they began to move towards the picnic tables laden with bounty from Cinnamon + Sugar.

Dane nodded, his gaze still focused on Jake's retreating form. "It's difficult when people won't take 'no' for an answer," he said. "But I don't think he'll be bothering you again, Hannah."

"Too right," agreed Sam, in a cheerful tone. "That bloke's just begging to have his legs broken to match the wrist."

"I call dibs on his right leg. You can break the left one," Hannah offered in a joking tone.

Maybe it was just her imagination, but it seemed that maybe Jake started walking a bit faster towards the first-aid trailer.

Dane shook his head, a wry smile tugging at his mouth.

"Try to keep the violence to PG-13, you two," he advised, taking the lasagna pan from Hannah before heading over to the picnic table to greet his wife.

Hannah waited a few moments until her cousin had moved far enough away to give her the illusion of privacy.

Then she said to Sam, "Hey, thanks for coming to my rescue. I was two seconds away from dropping your dinner and clocking Mr. Grabby Hands."

Sam recoiled. "What, and ruin our tea because of that yobbo? That would've been a waste of perfectly good food."

"I agree," Hannah said, still fighting the urge to move in and stand a lot closer to the big Aussie shifter. "So, you totally saved the day. And dinner."

Sam grinned down at her, his teeth white against his sooty face. "I actually came over because I wanted to ask you a favor. And see you again, of course," he added, hastily.

He squeezed her shoulder, then, disappointingly, withdrew his hand.

"Sure," Hannah said instantly. "I owe you one. How can I help?"

5

LOST AND FOUND

Sam handed her his phone. "Do you recognize this dog?"

Hannah looked down at the screen and saw a photo of a bedraggled, sad-eyed dog, most of his fur singed away. He was wrapped in a blanket and lying on what looked like a vehicle bench seat.

She felt an instant surge of sympathy for the pup. Poor little guy! I bet his people are worried to death about him. "Where did you find him?"

"Near a burned house along Eagle Creek Road. He was just sitting in the middle of road, like he was waiting for someone. Came right over to us when he saw us walking up. Seems like a sweet little fella."

Hannah frowned down at the phone. "Eagle Creek Road? I think this might be the Harper family's dog Edgar, but it's hard to tell. Let me ask Kayla...Edgar's one of her patients."

"Oh yeah, someone mentioned your sister was a vet," Sam said. "Go on, you can borrow my phone. I'm going to grab myself some of those choc chip biccies before they're all gone."

Hannah grinned up at him. "Annabeth and I made a couple of extra batches of cookies and turnovers this morning. We have a lot of experience dealing with hungry shifters."

Sam's eyes widened, and then his gaze turned hot and somehow predatory. "I bet you do."

Was that the barest hint of a growl in his deep voice?

Hannah felt an odd flutter in her chest. What was it about this Australian shifter that appealed to her so strongly? It wasn't just his rugged good looks. He was also refreshingly down-to-earth and really sweet.

He's the one. Her bear spoke up suddenly. *I want this one for our mate.*

Hannah felt like she'd just been jabbed by a cattle prod. Shock zinged through every nerve in her body, and she almost dropped Sam's phone. What are you talking about? I mean, he seems really nice, but we just met him!

"Hannah, are you all right?" Sam sounded concerned.

He's the one, her bear stated definitively. *Our mate. Don't let him get away.*

"Fine," Hannah managed. "I'm fine. Let me go ask Kayla about the dog."

Clutching his phone tightly, Hannah all but fled to find her sister.

~

Kayla was sitting at one of the picnic tables with their Swanson cousins Dane, Mark, Evan, Ash, and Tyler. At Hannah's approach, all of six of them looked up from their plates of lasagna, garlic bread, and salad.

"Hey Hannah, thanks so much for bringing dinner," Ash said, after hastily chewing and swallowing. "Is this Aunt Margaret's recipe?"

Hannah nodded. "She dropped by the bakery this afternoon to deliver it. Though these look like restaurant-sized pans, so I think Daniel might have had something to do with it."

Kayla's gaze darkened a little at the mention of the Bearpaw Springs Resort's executive chef, who was also their mother's new mate.

Hannah suppressed a sigh. She liked Daniel a lot, and had decided pretty quickly after meeting him that he qualified as Good People. Of course, the fact that they'd worked together to save a man's life at that first meeting had probably biased her in his favor.

But her older sister was still reserving judgment on the silver-haired sabertooth shifter, mainly because he was related to the notorious Pete Langlais, who had caused so much trouble at the ranch a good decade ago.

"So, you and Sam seem to have hit it off," Kayla said with a smirk. Apparently, she had decided not to comment on the possible origin of her dinner.

Hannah felt her cheeks flush with heat. "Um, he's really nice."

And sexy. And funny. And I could listen to his accent all day...

Apparently, her face was easy to read, because Kayla chuckled. "Good. He and the other Aussies have been awesome to work with. They've all got a great sense of humor, and they don't complain about the hard work."

"And Sam told us that his parents own a cattle ranch in Australia," Evan chimed in, grinning. "Think you might be able to convince him to move here? Dane could sure use a hand at our place, now that Mr. CEO Ash here is too busy to do his share of the chores."

"Hey!" protested Ash. "It's not my fault that our latest game is a big hit! It's all I can do to keep up with the demand for expansion modules."

"Um," Hannah said, uncomfortable at how excited her bear had gotten at the suggestion that Sam relocate to Bearpaw Ridge. *I just met him yesterday!* "Speaking of Sam, he and his guys apparently found a lost dog this afternoon. Do you think this might be Edgar? It's hard to tell with most of his fur gone."

Hoping that her cousins would take the hint to lay off the teasing her about Sam, she handed Kayla the phone.

Kayla studied the photo and nodded. "Oh yeah, that's him. See how ragged his left ear looks? Edgar had a run-in with something—probably a coyote—last autumn. I stitched up the worst of his injuries but his ear was mostly just cosmetic damage, and his fur usually covers it."

She handed the phone back to Hannah. "Erin and Ben will be so happy to see him." Her expression sobered. "Especially since they just lost their house and pretty much everything else."

"Everything except each other, that's what Erin told me this morning," Mark said quietly. "I'm helping them with the insurance claims. They'll rebuild, and we'll all pitch in to help them in whatever way we can. That's what we do here in Bearpaw Ridge."

"Edgar hightailed it out of the house while they were scrambling to get themselves and their most important papers in the car," Evan added. "Erin and Ben feared the worst, especially since the wind was pushing the fire so quickly up the hill."

"Hey, Miss Banana, my car is parked here," Kayla said. "You can borrow it if you like, and go return Edgar to the Harpers. They're staying with Teresa and Ernie at the dairy."

Hannah was preparing to ask *Why me?* when Kayla revealed her secret plan.

"Why don't you ask Sam to go with you? I'm sure he'd like a chance to see the parts of Bearpaw Ridge that aren't on fire right now."

"And don't forget to ask him if he might be interested in moving here," Evan added in a teasing tone.

6

FIRST DATE

As she drove Kayla's Subaru station wagon out to the Ornelas Organic Dairy, where Erin and Ben Harper would be staying until their house could be rebuilt, Hannah found herself sneaking sideways looks at Sam.

He'd eagerly accepted her invitation to help reunite Edgar with his family. Now, he sat next to Hannah in the Subaru's passenger seat, holding Edgar securely on his lap. He stroked the dog and scratched gently behind his floppy singed ears as he studied the passing landscape with interest.

Despite the brown sky and copper sun, the valley was still beautiful, filled with lush green pastures and fields. The highway followed the course of the Salmon River, its swiftly-flowing waters as clear as glass and its banks lined with tall cottonwood trees and bushy willows.

Sam's fellow firefighters had conspicuously declined to join them when she invited them along out of politeness.

Apparently, it wasn't only the Swansons who were trying to matchmake the two of them. Hannah didn't know whether to be overjoyed that everyone seemed to like Sam as much as she did, or mortified that her attraction to him was apparently about as subtle as a highway billboard.

Jake's comment about knowing that Hannah hadn't been able to find any dates lately had stung more than she had expected. *I mean, why do I even care what that jerk thinks?*

But after a few months of dud dates arranged through her ShiftMatch account, she had started wondering if she might be one of those shifters who never found a mate of their own.

No matter how good her prospective matches looked online, there had been zero chemistry between them when they met in person. And her bear's reactions to her dates had ranged from utter indifference to active rejection.

As if somehow sensing her dark turn of thought, Sam stopped petting Edgar. He reached over and took her right hand.

Just like his hand on her shoulder earlier, his touch felt simultaneously thrilling and comforting.

Sam's warm look full of masculine appreciation felt like a soothing balm on the lash of Jake's nasty comment.

"I'm still getting used to the steering wheel being on the wrong side of the car," he commented. "Back home, if I were sitting here, I'd be in the driver's seat right now."

Hannah laughed. "It would feel really strange to drive on the other side of the road."

She tried to imagine what Australia was like. All that came to mind were kangaroos and crocodiles. *And spiders. Really big spiders.*

Sam shook his head. "Oh, it's not the driving straight ahead part that trips you up," he advised. "It's making turns that's confusing. After we landed in Missoula and a hotel shuttle picked us up, I was convinced that we were going to have a head-on collision turning into the hotel's car park." He paused. "So, Kayla's your older sister? Do you have any other brothers or sisters?"

"I have an older brother. His name is Patrick, and he lives in Alaska, so I don't see him very often," Hannah said with a pang. "How about you? Any brothers or sisters?"

Sam shook his head. "I was a right terror as a kid. I think my Mum and Dad decided not to have any more after me. They worried that Oz might not survive more than one of us." His tone was gently self-deprecating, and he grinned at her. "That means I'm the heir apparent to a fair-sized cattle station about an hour's drive from Toowoomba. Have you ever been to Oz?"

"I've never been further away from home than Washington State, and only because Kayla went to veterinary school there,"

Hannah confessed. "I'd love to visit Patrick and Jessica in Alaska someday, but the problem is that they usually spend summers working on a dinosaur dig somewhere in the middle of nowhere, and by the time they get back to Anchorage, it's almost winter. And then there's my job here...Annabeth's got two kids, so she counts on me to run things when she can't be at work."

Sam nodded. "I feel guilty about not staying closer to home, especially now that Dad's getting older. They were a bit upset with me when I decided to become a firefighter and move to Gumdale on the coast—it's a suburb of Brisbane." He looked out the car's windows. "This place reminds me a bit of home, with all the hills and the trees. Even if they're not gum trees."

The nature programs that Hannah grown up watching had made Australia seem a giant red desert with kangaroos hopping around. She'd never imagined that it might look like home.

She couldn't help asking, "But are there kangaroos?"

Sam laughed. "Yeah. Lots of 'em. And wallabies, too. They come out at dusk and dawn to feed in our pastures."

"Just like the deer and elk here!" she said, surprised. "They seem to know that they can't be hunted near town, so there are always lots of them around at sunrise and sunset."

Sam nodded. "Yeah. And we've even got a few koalas living in the gum trees near the stream. If you came to visit, I could show them to you." His tone was hopeful, and it kindled a flutter of warm excitement deep inside Hannah's gut.

She spotted the sign for the Ornelas Organic Dairy just up ahead. "We're almost here, Edgar," she said, addressing the dog sitting patiently on Sam's lap. "I bet Erin and Ben are going to be really happy to see you."

~

There were tears of joy at the family's reunion with their beloved pet.

"I felt so guilty for leaving without him," Erin said.

The pretty blonde Ordinary woman was kneeling on the lawn in front of Ernie and Teresa Ornelas' big new house, her tears mixed with giggles as Edgar did his best to lick the salty drops from her face.

Her husband Ben, a big bear shifter with dark auburn hair and a bushy red beard, added, "But we couldn't stay any longer. The fire was moving so fast, we thought it might reach the road and cut us off."

He stood next to his mate, discreetly wiping away a few tears of his own as he watched the reunion.

Hannah had met the couple several times before, since Ben was a wildlife biologist who worked with her cousin Evan at the Idaho Fish and Game office in town, and Erin was a botanist working on a federal project studying the effects of climate change on the state's high-altitude vegetation.

Hannah smiled at them, happy for a little good news amid all of the tragic losses that this huge fire had inflicted over the past few days. "Well, I'm so happy that we could reunite you. We have to get going, though. I promised Sam that I'd treat him to some real American barbecue before I drove him back to the firefighting camp."

The white lie escaped her mouth before she had a chance to think about it. She glanced nervously at Sam for his reaction, and saw that the tall shifter was grinning down at her, his blue eyes sparkling.

"Yeah, my mates back at the camp are dead jealous that I'm goin' on a dinner date with a beautiful Yank," he said, happily. "Shall we?"

∼

"I'm sorry about just blurting the thing about dinner like that," Hannah apologized twenty minutes later. "I don't know what came over me."

They had just been seated at Justin Long's Wildcat Springs Texas BBQ restaurant on Main Street. Hannah had decided to bring Sam here to give him a quintessentially American experience. Plus, the food was outstanding.

The whole place was decorated in a rustic style, with wooden tables and chairs, and floors made from wide, weathered pine boards.

Sam seemed suitably impressed by the large collection of Texas-themed memorabilia covering the exposed brick side walls of the restaurant's interior. There were framed vintage black-and-white photos of the town of Wildcat Springs, located in the Hill Country near Austin, along with lariats, an assortment of cowboy hats, vintage Texas license plates, coils of barbed wire, spurs, antique saddles, and even a stuffed armadillo.

Sam and Hannah were each holding menus and their wolf shifter server Ethan Jacobsen had departed to pour them a couple of Brown Bear Ales from the restaurant's bar.

Sam waggled his dark gold eyebrows at her in an exaggerated leer. "Oi just love it when a sheila can't control herself around me," he intoned, deliberately exaggerating his Australian accent for comic effect.

Hannah laughed just as Ethan Jacobsen returned with their drinks.

"Your meals and drinks are on the house tonight," Ethan informed them. "Justin told us that he won't accept any money from the firefighters who came here to help out."

"I guess just I'll be paying for my own dinner then," Hannah said, cheerfully. "That's really nice of Justin."

Ethan frowned down at her. "And I know that you and Annabeth have been working your butts off to feed the fire crews," he said. "Justin will blow his top if he hears that I charged you anything."

"That's incredibly generous," Hannah replied, touched to the core. "I'll have to thank Justin when I see him."

He was her uncle-by-marriage, so she usually saw him at least once a week, at Aunt Elle's Sunday dinners.

Sam asked her a few questions about some of the menu items, and declared that he was starving, since he'd only managed to snatch a couple of cookies while back at camp, so they ordered one of the enormous Wildcat Springs Special sampler platters to share.

After placing their order, Sam raised his glass of dark amber ale and toasted her. "To pretty Yank bakers and their choc chip biccies."

Hannah grinned and raised her glass in return. "To hunky Aussie firefighters and their cute accents from Down Under," she intoned as solemnly as she could.

They touched glasses and drank.

"Accent? What accent? *I* don't have an accent," Sam informed her, putting his glass down on the table and wiping the foam from his mouth. "You lot are the ones who talk funny. As you'll discover when you come to visit me." He paused. "I think your Yank accent is pretty cute myself."

He wants to keep seeing me! An intoxicating wave of happiness rose from Hannah's middle.

"But I don't even have a passport," she protested, smiling.

"That's an easy problem to solve, innit?" Sam leaned back, studying her. "So, tell me about that wanker back at the camp. Mr. Grabby Hands. Is he your ex?"

"Oh, hell no," Hannah replied with an exaggerated shudder. "We went on one date. That was plenty for me. Would you believe that he demanded an explanation about why I didn't want to see him again, and then tried to argue with me when I told him that I didn't think we were a good match?" She shook her head in remembered disbelief. "I mean, why? Did he think I was going to date him again if he won the argument?"

Instead of taking Jake's bait, she had blocked without a further reply. At the time, she'd felt a tiny twinge of guilt that she was being rude, but mostly she had just felt relief at not having to deal with him again.

"Well, that's good. I mean, that you two weren't serious or anything," Sam amended hastily.

"Everyone was disappointed that things didn't work out," Hannah said. "I had a couple of friends ask me if maybe I wasn't being too picky."

"And why shouldn't you be picky when it comes to choosing a mate?" Sam demanded. "It's a lifetime commitment, after all." He shook his head and added, "And what kind of friends would want you to settle for a yobbo like Grabby Hands? He doesn't deserve someone like you!"

"But—" Hannah began to protest, both flattered and unsettled by Sam's unexpectedly passionate reaction to her story.

She also wanted to ask what the heck a *yobbo* was, but Sam wasn't done speaking. "Never undervalue yourself, Hannah. You deserve everything, and more."

"It's not like there are a ton of eligible bear shifter bachelors who live within driving distance of Bearpaw Ridge," Hannah tried to explain. "I mean, there's a lot of us in this area, but I'm related to most of them." She wrinkled her nose.

"So, does that mean I've got a chance? I know for sure that I'm not related to you." Sam's intensity dialed down as his grin returned.

Yes! Her bear all but shouted this, startling her.

"Maybe," Hannah said coyly.

She picked up her ale and drank, mostly to keep from staring at Sam. The more time she spent with him, the more she found herself liking him. He seemed completely unaware of how hot he was, and she loved his gentle sense of humor.

"And at least you've got a decent number of other shifters in these parts," Sam continued. "My family are the only bear shifters in the Darling Downs. There are a few other shifter families on the east coast, but they're located hundreds of kilometers away, in northern New South Wales and in Far North Queensland. Not exactly convenient for a coffee date, if you know what I mean."

Hannah nodded in sympathy.

"That's one of the reasons I applied for the job with Queensland Fire and Rescue Services. It was a good reason to move to the Brisbane area. Before I came here, I thought I was going to have to ask ShiftMatch for an arranged mating."

No! Hannah felt a sudden, weird pang at the thought of Sam Wilson getting mated via a traditional arranged match.

"I've got a ShiftMatch account, too," Hannah admitted. "That's how I met Jake. He actually lives in Montana, about a four-hour drive away. That was part of the problem with our first date. He thought he'd at least get laid, so he was pretty annoyed about driving all the way over here to meet me, and then..." She let her hand fall limply to the tabletop, mimicking a bird shot out of the sky. "Splat. Dud."

Ethan returned with an enormous oval platter heaped high with sliced brisket, grilled sausages, and pieces of BBQ chicken. The delectable smell of mesquite smoke rose from the platter, mingled with savory scents from the generous selection of side dishes held in a row of white crocks on the platter's perimeter. One crock held a generous portion of Justin's house-made barbecue sauce. The rest were filled with an assortment of coleslaw, beans, and mac-and-cheese.

"Enjoy your meal," Ethan said as he lowered the platter to the middle of the table. "I'll be right back with the cornbread and honey butter. And don't forget to leave room for dessert. It's included with the sampler platter."

Hannah and Sam dug in to the feast.

She was starving—lunchtime had been a long time ago, and she and Annabeth had worked hard to prepare and bake all of the extra goodies for the firefighters.

Sam looked like he was impressed with everything he put in his mouth.

The conversation went on hiatus for a short while as they each gave the excellent food their full attention.

At last, the bounty had been reduced to bones and empty crocks standing among a few smears of sauce. Sam surveyed the demolished platter with a satisfied expression. "That was some outstanding tucker."

"Just wait until you try the banana pudding. My whole family loves Justin's food," Hannah said. "He's originally from Texas, but he moved here after he mated my Aunt Elle." She drank the last of her ale. "I know you haven't had a chance to do much here except work, but what do you think of the US so far?"

"It's great. I love it," Sam assured her. "The drive down from Missoula to Bearpaw Ridge was beautiful, and most of the 'firies' I've met here are great, especially your cousins. I feel like we're all good mates now."

He reached across the table and took her hand. That same exciting jolt of contact that she'd felt earlier ran up her arm now.

"I'm really glad you invited me along to meet the Harpers and to go out on this date." He lowered his gaze, studying their linked hands, and she noticed that he had long, honey-colored lashes.

"I'll be honest with you, Hannah—I've been feeling a little down over the past few days, but spending time with you has cheered me right up."

"Did something happen?" she asked, concerned. She gave his hand a comforting squeeze.

Sam shook his head. "Oh, no, it's nothing anyone did, and I'm sure it'll all turn out right. It's just...well, you know that the seasons are reversed in the Southern Hemisphere, yeah?"

Hannah nodded, curious to hear what he had to say. His thumb stroked the back of her hand, causing interesting frissons of sensation.

"Well, as long as I can remember, my family's celebrated Christmas in July, because that's winter in Oz...not that Queensland ever gets cold, mind you. It's semi-tropical and we only have two real seasons—the Wet and the Dry. So, anyhow, this'll be the first year that I've ever missed my family's 'Christmas in July' dinner."

"I'm sorry—" she began, but his fingers tightened around her hand.

"No worries. Being here with you pretty much makes up for everything." He sounded sincere. "This is a better Christmas dinner than I ever hoped for."

Then he raised her hand to his lips and kissed her knuckles. His lips were warm and soft, and their touch sent a bolt of heat searing along every nerve down to the pit of her belly.

He felt it, too. His blue eyes grew hot, and she saw a hint of shifter gold in their depths.

Oh my God. I want him so badly, and all we're doing is holding hands! Hannah cleared her throat. "Um, can I show you my favorite place? It's just a short drive—"

She stopped speaking because Ethan returned to their table. He held a tray with two bowls of creamy vanilla pudding topped with fresh sliced bananas over a base of crisp Nilla Wafers.

His gaze fastened on Hannah and Sam's joined hands and Hannah knew that everyone in town would hear about her date with Sam by tomorrow morning, at the very latest.

Hannah reflexively tried to pull away her hand, but Sam maintained a firm but gentle grip. Which was okay with her, because she didn't really want to lose his touch.

"Hope you left room for dessert," Ethan said cheerfully, putting the banana pudding on the table. Then he began piling their dinner plates and silverware on the platter in preparation for clearing everything away.

"Hey, mate, would you mind putting those in a takeaway box for us?" Sam asked, indicating the bowls of pudding. "We've got some plans that can't wait."

He reached into his jeans pocket and pulled out a wad of bills. He counted out a generous tip one-handed and tried to hand the bills to Ethan.

Ethan waved away the money. "Like I said, your money's no good here. Your Australian crew saved my dad's barn and his prize stud yesterday. His ranch is the one right off Wolf Run Road."

Sam nodded. "That was a close call, right enough. And your dad has some fine horses on his place."

"Yeah," Ethan agreed. "We can't thank you enough." He winked at Hannah, and she felt her face grow hot. "Enjoy the rest of your evening."

7

POSSUM

A bout three miles out of town. Hannah spotted what she was looking for: a large brown sign labeled "Public Access Area," with fish and boat symbols, and an arrow pointing at a sloping driveway leading off the raised highway embankment.

She carefully turned the big station wagon onto the narrow driveway, and bumped down a narrow gravel lane that led into a dense grove of trees on the riverbank.

"This is your favorite place in Bearpaw Ridge?" Sam asked, sounding a little incredulous as he looked around.

"Well, it used to be my favorite place when I was in high school," Hannah informed him. "I haven't been here in a while."

Her heart pounded with anticipation, and she couldn't believe how much just having her knuckles kissed had turned her on.

Sam just looked puzzled, so she added, "I used to take my dates here when I wanted to spend some time with them without everyone in town knowing where I was and what I was doing."

"Oh. I see." Sam's eyes widened in comprehension.

Just as she remembered, there was a small dirt parking lot in the middle of the grove, with picnic tables and a boat ramp leading down into the river.

And just as she'd hoped, the parking lot and picnic area were completely deserted. Summer days were long in Bearpaw Ridge, and there was still at least an hour or two of daylight left, but all of the fishermen and kayakers had apparently decided to head home for the day.

Or maybe the smoky skies had discouraged them from venturing out at all.

Hannah parked and climbed out of the station wagon. She had barely closed her car door when Sam pushed her up against the side of the car.

He pinned her with his hips, hands tangled in her hair as he bent and captured her mouth in a hard kiss that was passionate, a little rough, and totally hot.

Hannah heard herself make a sound of pure need deep in her throat. She grabbed at his densely-muscled shoulders and pressed herself against him, feeling the hard bulge of his erection behind the thick fabric of his jeans.

Her hands dropped to roam freely over his sides and back, exploring him through the barrier of cloth stretched smooth and taut over ridges of hard muscle.

Sam's hands moved as well, slipping under her hair to stroke her nape before moving down to trace the long line of her spine. He cradled her ass in his big hands, pulling her ever tighter against him. And he never stopped kissing her, their tongues waging a sensual war that made victors of them both.

Sam drew back a little, his breath coming fast. "I want you, Hannah," he said, his voice rough as his bear rose up inside him, gilding his eyes. "I want you to be mine."

That *mine* sent a thrill through her.

Yes! Her bear enthusiastically agreed.

He leaned in for another kiss. Hannah was more than okay with that...until she remembered something very important she needed to tell him.

She stiffened in his embrace and turned her head away to speak.

Unlike Jake, Sam respected her body language. He stopped immediately and pulled back, though she could feel the tension of desire singing through his body like a live wire.

"I'm not on any birth control right now." *If only I'd known that my meal delivery run with Annabeth would turn into a date with the hottest bear shifter I've ever met!*

He froze. "Bloody hell. I wasn't expecting that we'd—I mean, I didn't bring anything—"

She silenced him with a quick kiss. Her blood ran hot in her veins, and the place between her legs felt swollen and aching with desire for him. "That just means we'll have to be a little creative."

She reached between them and stroked the hard bulge pushing against the front of his jeans.

"Creative," he said, sounding short of breath. "Oi, I like the sound of that."

She grinned at him. Then he drove all thought out of her mind by cupping her breasts through her Cinnamon + Sugar t-shirt.

He caressed her sensitive nipples with his thumbs, so that they stiffened and became visible even through her bra and top.

Her smoldering desire flared even hotter at his teasing touch.

Desperate to get him naked as quickly as possible, she yanked his Queensland Fire and Rescue t-shirt up out of his jeans.

He took a half-step back and raised his arms, smiling down at her.

I really should take my time and enjoy this, Hannah thought, but she wanted him much too badly to go slowly.

It was all she could do not to tear off his clothes.

She got his t-shirt off and tossed it on a nearby picnic table. She couldn't help running her hands over his bared torso, relishing the feeling of his heated skin against her palms, and the soft, springy, light brown hair sprinkled over his broad chest and muscled abs.

"You are so hot," she said fervently.

He grinned, but she saw a flush rising from his collarbones and creeping up his tanned golden skin of his throat. "You're not half-bad yourself, possum."

Hannah drew back slightly and scowled up at him in mock indignation, though her hands remained plastered firmly to his heated skin.

"Did you just call me a possum?" she asked indignantly. "As in, the critter that looks like a giant white rat and plays dead?"

Sam grimaced and shook his head. "Our Aussie possums are cute, I swear to you. All big eyes and adorable furry faces. Here, let me show you—" He reached for the phone tucked in his jeans pocket, but Hannah grabbed his hand and put it firmly on her breast.

He laughed, then went very still as she reached for the waist of his jeans.

"I feel like you've been spying on my dreams of the past few couple nights," he said, sounding a little breathless.

She grinned at him, moved her hands to his hips, and slowly sank down to her knees. "Shoes first," she said primly.

Luckily for her, he'd changed out of his firefighter's boots and into sneakers before they'd left on their mission to reunite Edgar with his family.

Sam groaned but let her unlace them and pull them off before she reached up to deal with his jeans.

She unbuttoned them, then pulled them and his briefs down to his ankles. His thick cock sprang free, erect and ready for action.

Hannah leaned forward to place a playful kiss on the broad, hard shaft. It felt smooth and burning-hot against her lips.

Sam groaned again and pulled her up with his effortless strength.

"My turn now," he informed her.

He all but tore off her brown-and-pink Cinnamon + Sugar t-shirt and the plain cotton bra underneath. His urgency sent a thrill through her. She loved that he obviously wanted her as badly as she wanted him right now.

He kissed and nibbled his way down her throat to her bared breasts with frantic hunger, as she clutched at his shoulders and arched, offering herself to him.

He bit her nipples just hard enough to send a jolt of pure pleasure straight to her pussy, then sucked the sensitized tips hard between his lips, making her moan with each teasing flick of his tongue.

It was driving her crazy with sheer, mind-blowing arousal, and she felt as if she was going to either explode or lose her mind.

She went up on her tiptoes and tilted her hips, desperate to get some relief from the throbbing, intense ache between her legs.

Sam held her at bay with an unbreakable grip as he continued to torment her breasts.

"Sam...please," she begged, finally, which seemed to be the signal he'd been waiting for.

His hands under her ass, he stepped neatly out of the crumpled pile of jeans and briefs on the ground, lifted her effortlessly, and carried her over to the nearest picnic table.

He bent to kiss her again, his mouth was hard and urgent, and when she wrapped her legs around his hips, she felt his hard cock pushing against her aching pussy through her jeans.

"Oh God, I want you so badly!" she panted.

He lowered her to the tabletop. She felt him unzip her jeans and eagerly helped him push them down. One arm circled her waist, supporting her, while his free hand slid down the front of her panties.

Hannah moaned as she felt his fingers slip between the hot, wet folds of her pussy.

"Please, Sam," she begged, utterly shameless now.

"You feel so good," he whispered, slowly circling her clit with his fingertip.

She moaned with desperate need and reached for the hard length of his erection, cupping in her fingers. "I'm so close...please..."

"Oh, yeah, I'm going to make you come," he said hoarsely. "I want to hear you."

"Yes! Please..." She tilted her hips, pushing herself against his hand, as she fisted his hot, hard shaft.

She drew her hand up his length in a slow caress, thumbing the broad, smooth head.

The breath shuddered out of him as he continued to tease her swollen, sensitive clit with just the right amount of pressure, each brush of his fingers sending electric jolts through her.

She was so close...she just needed a little more....

"Sam...please...," she begged in a fierce whisper, speeding up her own caresses, enjoying his own gasps and groans of pleasure as she worked his cock.

He pushed a finger inside her, then another, then a third, stretching her in an indescribably pleasurable way. She spread her legs eagerly for him and moaned, feeling the edge of the picnic table pressing against her ass.

"I love it that you want me as badly as I want you right now," he murmured.

Sam pulled his fingers partway out of her and thrust them back in, making her moan as they rubbed tantalizingly against her aroused nerves. He began to move, using his thumb to rub her clit every time he worked his fingers in and out of her slick, hungry entrance.

Hannah imagined it was his hard cock driving into her and felt her climax gathering like a storm.

Sam kissed her, drinking in the soft sounds she was making.

"You are so beautiful and sexy," he whispered between kisses. "I love touching you, Hannah, love making you feel good."

He picked up the pace of his thrusts, and she writhed around his fingers, arching against the delicious friction he was generating. She was so close now...just a little more...

Sam bent, and she felt his sharp teeth close on her throat, a growl vibrating against her skin.

It was enough to send her over the edge.

Her fingers loosened around his shaft as she momentarily forgot about everything except the pleasure exploding through her like a lightning strike on water. Ripples of intense pleasure coursed through her body, making her writhe helplessly against his hand.

Hannah drew a shuddering breath and buried her face against his shoulder, muffling the sounds she made as she pulsed around Sam's impaling fingers. She felt like she was drowning in a sea of exquisite sensations.

He kissed her, his tongue taking possession of her mouth as he continued to caress her, drawing out her climax in wave after wave of pleasure.

Sam gentled his touch, withdrawing his fingers as Hannah began to come down from her peak. He continued to stroke her clit lightly, summoning every last splash of sensation.

When her orgasm had subsided at last, she slumped against him, feeling dizzy and drunk on pleasure. His arms wrapped around him, holding her close against his bare, warm body, and his strong heartbeat hammered against her cheek.

Eventually, though, she became aware that she'd just left him hanging.

Hannah turned her face into his chest and kissed it.

"Your turn," she murmured before sliding off the picnic table.

Her knees felt like jelly as she guided him to switch places.

Panting with unquenched desire, Sam obeyed without protest, seating himself on the table and leaning back on his hands.

Hannah stepped between his knees and gave him a long, lingering kiss before she began to work her way down his body, tasting every inch of his throat, chest, and those lovely defined abs.

"Your mouth is so beautiful," Sam told her, his hands sliding into her unbound hair to cradle her head. "I've been dreaming about doing this with you...what it would be like to have your sweet lips wrapped around my cock."

"I really wish we could go all the way today. But I'll try to make you feel as good as you just made me feel," Hannah said, as she bent and teased his erect cock by blowing on it.

Sam groaned and she felt his hands tighten in her hair.

But he didn't try to force her head down, though she could tell how much the effort at restraint was costing him. It excited her and rekindled her arousal.

She opened her mouth and licked him, a long, wet stroke that lingered and swirled around his tip.

He thrust his hips upwards in what looked like an involuntary reaction, trying to fuck her mouth, so she closed her fist around the base of his thick shaft and took back control.

Sam groaned loudly as she closed her lips around the broad tip of his cock. She played with it, letting the head slide against the ridged roof of her mouth, then used her tongue to tease his sensitive slit, tasting the salt and musk.

He shuddered and gasped when she began to gently stroke the heavy sac between his legs.

"Do that again. Please," he gasped.

She giggled, pleased at his reaction, and obeyed, taking as much of him in her mouth as she could.

She moaned softly around his cock, caressing him with the sound, and swallowed him to the hilt before dragging her lips and tongue up his rigid shaft.

Sam shuddered beneath her and swore incoherently. Pleased with his reaction, she repeated the caress again and again, drinking in his reactions as she sensed him getting close to his own finish.

Then he growled and convulsed, filling her mouth with the taste of salt as he shook beneath her.

Hannah swallowed everything he gave her, guiding him tenderly through his climax to his completion, until he sprawled back on the table, sweaty and sticky and with the sweetest, happiest smile on his face.

She wiped her mouth and crawled up on the table with him. He gathered her in with one arm and drew her to drape herself over his chest. They cuddled together for a while, listening to the same wind that was whipping the wildfires into a frenzy a few miles away rustle the leaves of the trees above them here.

"How about we go for a swim?" he suggested eventually, when his heartbeat had slowed to its normal, steady rhythm again.

She looked at him doubtfully. "We're out of sight of the highway and the bridge here, but once we get in the water...well, I'm not thrilled about flashing every pickup that roars by."

"Then let's wear our other shapes," Sam suggested. "It's not bear-hunting season or anything, is it?"

Hannah shook her head. "No one's allowed to shoot game this close to town, anyway." The thought of letting her bear out to play in the cool, refreshing waters of the river was a tempting one. "Okay."

Her bear rose eagerly to the surface, sending a sharp prickling sensation over her skin like a wave of goosebumps.

They scrambled off the table and quickly shifted to their other shapes.

When they were done, Kayla paused to admire Sam's bear.

He was a huge grizzly with honey-colored fur that matched his human hair color, and golden shifter eyes. She was not a petite bear herself, but standing next to him, he made her feel small.

He looked her over in turn, then leaned in to touch noses with an approving huff before turning to gallop swiftly in the direction of the boat ramp.

Feeling happier than she could remember, Hannah raced after him, determined not to let him win the race to the water's edge.

8

HOT TO HANDLE

The next week was the happiest that Hannah could remember.

She and Annabeth worked long shifts at the bakery seven days a week, preparing meals for the volunteers of the Bearpaw Ridge Fire Department and the visiting Queensland Fire and Rescue firefighters that Dane and the others had informally adopted as their own.

And she and Sam spent every free moment together, both of them sacrificing precious sleep in favor of more rewarding and pleasurable activities.

The more time she spent with the Aussie bear shifter, the more she liked him, and the more she craved his kisses...and other things.

The grueling efforts of the assembled firefighting forces to dig fire breaks and clear defensible perimeters around vulnerable buildings on the outskirts of town began to pay off.

Hannah and the other residents of Bearpaw Ridge and its outlying farms and ranches eagerly followed the daily fire-fighting progress reports that Dane issued via the BPRFD's Facebook page and Twitter feed.

25% contained...30% contained...40% contained.

Then the rains came, a strong and very wet storm that rolled in from the Pacific Northwest and drenched the entire state for two days.

And just like that, the town's weeks-long ordeal by smoke and flame ended.

The grateful residents of Bearpaw Ridge quickly organized a huge "Thank You" celebration that included live music, catered food and drinks donated by every restaurant and pub in the area, and large party tents to keep everyone dry.

Hannah and Sam sat together in one corner of the live music tent, their feet tapping as they listened to a talented country music band performing with fiddle, mandolin, guitar, and bass.

They held hands with almost desperate fervor. Hannah was acutely aware that the quenching of the enormous and destructive wildfire also meant that the mutual-aid fire crews would be heading back to their homes very soon.

"Hey," she said softly, leaning into the tall Aussie sitting next to her. "Do you want to come home with me rather than going back to the camp tonight?"

"You know I do," Sam replied. "But I'm on cleanup duty at dawn." He grimaced, and Hannah saw the shadows of fatigue on his face.

Everyone involved in fighting the fire was bone-deep tired, but victory had given them all an extra boost of energy, so they danced and celebrated and enjoyed the temporary surcease.

Tomorrow, the grim task of assessing damage and conducting mop-up operations would begin. But for tonight, everyone was taking a well-deserved break to enjoy some good food and good music.

"That's all right," Hannah assured him. "I have to be at the bakery in time to open it at 5:00 a.m. I promise I'll get you back to the camp in plenty of time."

Sam gave her a slow, sweet smile. "I reckon neither of us are getting much sleep tonight."

"I sure hope not," Hannah replied fervently.

She rose, and Sam followed her eagerly.

She waved at Kayla on her way out. Her sister, who was dancing with fellow firefighter Michael Jacobsen, waved back and gave her a thumbs-up.

Kayla had made it very clear that she liked and approved of Sam, and hoped that Kayla might be able to talk him into staying in Bearpaw Ridge.

Tonight's the night I ask him to stay, Hannah thought, as she and Sam left the tent and ran through the pouring rain to where she'd parked her pickup, which Sam charmingly referred to as her "ute."

∽

Why am I so nervous about asking him? Kayla asked herself as she pulled up in front of the Queen Anne Victorian house on the Grizzly Creek Ranch.

She and Kayla had moved in to the lovely old house last autumn, right after their mom had moved out to go live at the Cougar Lake Ranch with her new mate Daniel Langlais.

Because it'll kill me if he says no.

He won't say no, her bear assured her. It sounded a lot more confident than Hannah felt.

She'd meant to ask Sam during the drive from town, but had chickened out and instead had asked him a bunch of questions about what it was like growing up on his parents' cattle station.

His answers made it sound like his childhood had been a lot like hers, minus the benefits of living in a shifter community.

She opened the door to her home and ushered him inside.

"Alone at last," she said, shutting the front door behind them. "Kayla won't be home for hours, maybe not at all."

"Well, in that case..." Sam bent to kiss her, then swung her up into his arms.

He carried her through a large cased opening into the living room, which was furnished with a selection of Victorian furniture that had come with the house. It wasn't really to Hannah or Kayla's taste, but the two of them hadn't yet gotten around to figuring out what they wanted instead.

Sam made a beeline for the huge Victorian horsehair sofa. He lowered her to it, and slid the hem of her new sundress up her thighs, revealing the new, lacy panties she'd bought for the occasion.

He paused to admire them.

"Nice knickers, possum," he told her, using the nickname he'd bestowed on her.

Hannah didn't mind. She had finally gotten around to looking up Australian possums, and discovered that they were every bit as cute and adorable as Sam had claimed.

Sam hooked his fingers under the lace, and pulled them down her legs. She eagerly lifted her hips to help him, then reached to unfasten the front of his jeans.

They finished undressing each other with breathless haste, scattering their clothes all around the sofa.

Sam retrieved a handful of condom packets from his jeans and brandished them triumphantly. "I came prepared to conquer this time," he informed her, grinning.

"I love a detail-oriented man," Hannah replied, eyeing his impressive erection with anticipation. She reached for him. "Allow me."

She took her time rolling the condom on him, caressing and teasing his hard, hot length.

"Enough," he growled finally, and lunged on top of her.

He covered her with his heavy body, devouring her mouth as his hands tangled in her long hair.

Hannah wound her arms around his neck and returned his kiss as every nerve in her body seemed to catch fire.

"I want you so badly." She wrapped her legs around his hips and reached between them, guiding the blunt head of his cock so that it pressed against her wet, aching entrance.

Sam moved into her with one powerful thrust, filling her completely.

"Oh. My. God," she gasped, relishing the way he stretched her. "Don't stop."

He took her fast and hard, his mouth covering hers, muffling her moans as he moved against her, his stiff length caressing her clit with every long thrust.

Her climax wound up rapidly, then released deep inside her, rocking her with powerful pulses of pleasure. Her climax went on and on without dying away, lifting her on blissful waves that rocked her into ecstasy.

She clung to Sam as his thrusts sped up and he went deeper and harder. He gasped against her lips, and she felt every muscle in his body tense as he came, his thrusts faltering and losing their rhythm.

When he was done, he rolled them both over, and held her draped across him, still firmly joined to him.

"Mine," he said, kissing her long and slow and deep, just as she liked.

Then he started moving under her, his cock still hard. Hannah pushed herself up and prepared to enjoy the ride, relishing the solid strength of him between her legs as she moved in rhythm with his thrusts.

This time, his movements were slow and deep as he drove her to a second climax before coming himself.

"Mine," he said again, as she collapsed on top of him. "I want you to be mine, Hannah."

"Yeah," she agreed and received a breathtakingly sweet smile in return.

He cuddled with her for a bit, rekindling her arousal with teasing caresses over her sensitized breasts.

Then he urged her up and off the couch. He sat up and put her on his lap, sliding her down onto his renewed erection. She straddled his legs while he took her from behind. It was raw and animalistic, his fingers digging into her hips as he went even deeper than before.

She gasped and writhed and quickly found herself coming again.

A brief respite of kissing, then, unbelievably, he was ready to go again. This time they spooned together on the sofa, his hands cupping her breasts as he moved against her.

When he came, thrusting up into her with a loud growl, he reached around her and stroked her to yet another climax.

She began realize that he hadn't been overly optimistic when he'd brought that many condoms on their date.

"God, I love shifter guys!" she panted, reaching back to pat his hip. She gathered up her courage and added, "I'm going to miss you so much when you go home, Sam."

He flattened his hand over her belly in a possessive gesture that made her melt inside. "I really wish I could stay." Her heart soared. Then he added, "Promise you'll come and visit me in Oz."

You have to make him stay with us! her bear ordered.

Hannah forced herself to laugh. *Keep it light. Don't scare him off.* "You might have to keep trying to convince me."

She turned in his arms to face him, and kissed him in a series of slow, teasing nibbles that traced the perimeter of his mouth. "Are you up to the challenge, Sam?"

"You know I am," he said, reaching up to tuck a long lock of her dark hair behind her ear. "Now, I want to hear you come for me again."

He rose above and proceeded to kiss and nip his way down her body until he reached her thighs.

He opened her knees wide and bent eagerly to pleasure her with his hot, hungry mouth as she bucked and writhed under the firm restraint of his hands.

"You taste delicious," he told her. "I don't ever want to stop doing this."

She came again and again, sobbing with almost unbearable pleasure as his lips and his tongue worked magic on her body.

Finally, when she was wrung out with pleasure and tucked against him on the sofa, he said, "I know we haven't known each other very long, but I don't want to leave you."

Her heart soared.

"I don't want you to leave, either. I've been trying to find a way to tell you without scaring you off," she confessed.

His low chuckle rumbled through her. "Ah, no worries, possum. You fed me and brought me home, so I reckon you're stuck with me now."

"I...I really like you." *More than just like, but how do I tell him that?*

"It's more than that for me, Hannah," he said roughly. "My bear has chosen you as our mate, and I'm fine with that."

Hannah wasn't surprised by the rush of joy that moved through her at his words. "So, you'll stay here, with me?"

Sam shook his head, his expression regretful. "I can't, Hannah. My parents are getting older, and they expect me to take over the station when they retire." He took a deep breath. "Come to Australia with me. You'll love it there, I swear to you."

Yes! Yes! Her bear was ecstatic. *He wants to be our mate!*

Hannah wasn't expecting the terror that came charging at joy's heels. She'd been dreaming of this day, wanted to be his mate... but she'd never considered leaving everything and everyone she knew behind to move to a different country. It was a huge change.

And I've never been farther from home than Seattle!

"I...my mom...Annabeth really relies on me to help her at the bakery..." The excuses tumbled out, propelled by her sense that she was standing on the edge of a cliff, knowing that she could never turn back if she decided to take a chance and step forward.

Mating between shifters was a forever commitment. That meant that moving to Australia, a place she'd never visited before, and one that was on the other side of the world, would also be a forever commitment

Sam expression was visibly disappointed. "I know it's a lot to ask, but I don't want to live without you, Hannah. Please tell me that you'll at least give it serious thought."

"I will," she promised. "I really will."

"We still have a few hours before I have to be back at camp. Show me your bedroom and let me do my best to convince you."

9

GUILT TRIP

B leary with lack of sleep, pleasantly sore, and wracked with indecision, Hannah drove Sam back to the firefighters' camp in the wee hours of the morning. They parted with lingering kisses made bittersweet by the cloud of his impending departure and her inability to commit to leaving her home and her family.

She dragged herself through her work at Cinnamon + Sugar until her shift ended at lunchtime. With a few hours remaining until she was due to help Annabeth deliver dinner to the firefighters, Hannah decided to drive out to the Cougar Lake Ranch and visit her mother.

She knew that Daniel would be at work, which was good. She wanted to have a private conversation with her mom.

"Hannah! What a nice surprise!" Margaret Swanson exclaimed as she opened the door of the newly-renovated ranch house that she shared with Daniel.

Hannah's mother was a tall woman with shoulder-length straight reddish-brown hair heavily frosted with silver, smooth skin bare of any makeup, and a warm smile. Crow's feet at the corners of her eyes and the smile lines bracketing her mouth enhanced the air of quiet strength and kindness that surrounded her.

She leaned forward to peer at Hannah. "Is everything all right, my dear?"

"Hi, Mom. I really need your advice about something," Hannah said.

Something in her expression must have betrayed the depths of her anguish, because she suddenly found herself folded into a soft hug. "Oh, my dear. Is this about the Australian firefighter that you've been seeing?"

Hannah nodded, her face still buried in her mother's shoulder as she held tight, breathing in Mom's familiar, comforting scent.

"Kayla told me that he's one of us, a bear shifter. She really likes him," Margaret said, drawing Hannah into the house. "Why don't I make us some tea, and then you can tell me all about it?"

～

The tea was her mom's favorite mint blend, and tasting it reminded Hannah of all the things that she'd miss if she moved away across the ocean.

They sat on the brand-new couch in the great room, with its floor-to-ceiling windows providing a stunning view over Cougar Lake and the densely forested hills that surrounded the lake.

Margaret and Daniel had bought all new furniture in a comfortable, contemporary rustic style that complimented the great room's rustic wood beams and vaulted ceilings.

Hannah found herself spilling her guts about meeting Sam, their whirlwind romance, and his proposal to her.

Margaret listened quietly, nodding occasionally. Hannah figured that her mom had heard quite a few of the details already— no secrets in a small town like Bearpaw Ridge— but Margaret's eyes widened when Hannah told her about Sam's proposal...and the fact that he was determined to continue living in Australia.

"...I think I'm in love with him. My bear wants him as our mate, but I don't know what to do!" Hannah finished, her voice rising with emotion.

Her mother's expression was troubled as she set aside her mug. "Australia? Oh dear, but that's so far away!"

"I know," Hannah said, miserably. She stared down at her tea as if hoping to divine answers from the patterns of rising steam.

"My dear, I know you have strong feelings for Sam," her mother said, gently. "But you really need to think this through. Do you really want to leave your home? And spend the rest of your life away from all of us?"

Her mother's words echoed the same doubts and questions that had been swirling around and around Hannah's head since last night.

"And what about grandchildren?" Margaret continued. "You know how much I miss Patrick, living so far away in Alaska. Seeing photos of Olivia by email and video chat isn't the same thing as being able to spend time with her and watch her grow up. It would break my heart if the same thing happened with your children, Hannah."

"But I love him!" Hannah's voice sounded very small.

Her mother smiled compassionately. "And I love you, my dear. I would miss you so much if you moved away to the other side of the ocean."

What do I do? How can I decide when I know that I'm going to hurt someone I love, no matter which course of action I take?

10

COLD FEET

" A re you sure you can't stay a little longer? Just a few more days?" Hannah begged Sam a few hours later.

She had returned from her visit with her mom feeling more conflicted than ever.

Then she and Annabeth had made their dinner run to the fire-fighter's camp, which was already emptying out.

Sam shook his head, and pulled her tightly against him. "We're flying out first thing in the morning. In fact, we've already packed up our gear and the tents, and we'll be driving to Missoula tonight."

"Oh no." Hannah couldn't believe that this was really goodbye. She'd been counting on having at least another few days to think about her decision. "Oh, God, Sam. I can't believe this! I'm going to miss you so much."

"Same here," he said into her hair.

She felt his warm breath against her neck and ear, maybe for the last time, and felt like crying with the unfairness of their situation.

"Have you had a chance to think about..." he began, then stopped. "God, Hannah, I don't want to live without you. Say you'll marry me and come to Australia to be my mate."

"I—" Hannah's throat felt so tight she could hardly breathe, much less talk. "I love you, Sam. I don't want to live without you, either, but it's such a big decision. I—I just need a little more time."

He tensed, and guilt stabbed through her. She added, "I really wish you could stay just a little longer, so that we could get to know each other better."

"I know what I want," he said, softly. "It's you. I'm in love with you, Hannah. If we're going to do this, I need to know that you feel the same way about me. But I can't stay. I'm so sorry...the flights, the visa, it would all be a huge mess."

"Is this the end?" Hannah asked, her eyes stinging with tears. Her vision blurred. "Have I messed up everything?"

She felt his lips on her temple, the corner of her eyes, her cheeks as he tried to kiss away her tears.

"Don't cry, my love," he begged. "You haven't messed anything up, I swear! If you can't come with me now, I promise I'll wait for you in Australia. Just don't make me wait too long. Please."

11

HEARTBROKEN

As he'd predicted, Sam Wilson and his fellow Aussies departed for Missoula and the first leg of their long journey home right after their final communal supper with the Bearpaw Ridge firefighters.

Tears streaming down her face, Hannah stood waving goodbye until the van carrying the Queensland Fire and Rescue team vanished from sight.

Sam's last, desperate kiss still burned against her mouth, and his scent still clung to her. Both would soon dissipate, leaving only memories.

He's gone. And he's not coming back. She felt numb with shock and disbelief, but she knew that the pain would set in soon.

It felt like that long-ago day when her mother, crying, had told her and Kayla and Patrick that their dad wasn't coming home from Iraq.

Inside, her bear was yowling with grief and frustration. *Why did he go away? He was supposed to be our mate!*

Her phone buzzed with an incoming text message. It was from Sam.

Miss you already.

Me too, she texted in reply. **Love you.**

I wish I'd been brave enough to tell him yes.

~

Afterwards, Hannah could only remember bits and pieces about the next two weeks.

She wanted to crawl in her bed and sleep away the days and nights, but she had to go to work. Most days, that routine was the only thing that kept her going.

The world had gone gray and joyless with Sam's departure. She moved through her tasks like a robot, waiting for that next text or photo that provided the only flecks of bright color in her life right now.

For him, Hannah forced herself to pretend that everything was okay, sending him selfies with the bakery as a backdrop, asking

Annabeth to take photos of her doing everyday things like making an espresso or rolling out dough for pastries.

But things weren't normal. For the first time in Hannah's life, her bear was gone. The constant companionable presence of her beast had dwindled to almost nothing.

Worried, Hannah tried to shift one evening. She couldn't do it. And she couldn't find a way to tell anyone. They couldn't help her, anyway.

Though they lived together in the same house, she and Kayla rarely saw each other, thanks to their wildly differing work schedules. Now that the fire was out, Kayla had returned to her regular job as a veterinarian, which had her driving out on urgent calls at all hours of the day and night.

And that was okay, because Hannah was barely managing to keep things together, and she didn't think she could bear her older sister's attempts at sympathy.

~

"Hannah, I'm worried about you," said Annabeth.

She was holding Hannah's phone and frowning down at the photo she'd just taken of Hannah slicing fresh nectarines for a tart.

"I'm fine," Hannah said automatically. It had become her standard response when anyone...her cousins, her mother, her friends...asked how she was doing.

Because she was pretty sure that no one wanted to hear about the fact that her heart had been ripped out of her chest and she was hollowed-out and hurting...and it was all her fault.

"No, you're not fine, and everyone can see it. I'm really worried about you. Here, put that down." Annabeth took the knife away from Hannah. "Let's sit down for a moment and have some coffee."

The breakfast and coffee crowd had come and gone, and the lunch crowd was still an hour away, so Cinnamon + Sugar was deserted at the moment. Hannah and Annabeth normally used this time to replenish the bakery cases and make the grab-n-go sandwiches that were stocked in the cooler.

Hannah filled a mug with some coffee and followed her boss out to the small collection of marble-topped tables and comfy chairs in the café section of the bakery. She stopped to add cream and sugar before taking a seat across from Annabeth.

Annabeth didn't try to interrogate her. She just sat there, sipping her coffee, letting her calm, kind presence work its magic on Hannah.

"I'm a coward. I messed up everything!" Hannah finally blurted out.

"What happened?" Annabeth asked, her voice gentle.

"Sam asked me to be his mate. But he says he can't move here, so I'd have to go to Australia. I...it was such a long way away... and then I talked to Mom and she looked so sad when she mentioned that she only saw Patrick and Jessica and Olivia for the holidays..."

Hannah realized that she was babbling out a stream of excuses, and reined herself in. When she spoke again, she reached deep inside her for the truth. "And I was freaked out about having to make such a big change without having any time to really plan for it."

Kayla would have gotten that impatient look on her face, and said something sarcastic about Hannah overthinking things.

But Annabeth just nodded. "I think I understand. When I came to Bearpaw Ridge, it was a pretty sudden decision. I'd finally realized that my relationship with my fiancé wasn't healthy, and I wanted to run away from my problems. My friend Maggie Ornelas told me about Bearpaw Ridge, and a bakery that needed a new owner..." She smiled wryly at Hannah. "All my life, I'd tried to make other people happy—my mother, Roger...well, everyone."

Hannah nodded, struck by an unexpected feeling of kinship with Annabeth. "Yeah, I get it."

As the youngest in her family, with two older siblings that acted like she annoyed them a lot of the time, and a grieving mother, Hannah had spent a lot of her childhood tiptoeing around, trying not to make a fuss. Hoping not to be noticed.

"I always felt like I was somehow an inconvenience to everyone around me, so I worked extra-hard to be nice and good and to twist myself into the shapes that other people drew for me,"

Annabeth said. "When I decided to leave my old life behind, it was really scary. I knew I was stepping out of the path that my mother and Roger had decided for me, and that they'd be really upset and really unhappy with me. I was so nervous in the days leading up to my departure that I couldn't sleep and I could barely eat. And I was petrified that Roger would somehow find out that I was leaving, and try to stop me."

She stopped speaking for a long moment, and stared down into the depths of her coffee cup. Her expression was distant, and a little sad.

"But you did it anyway," Hannah said, struck with newfound admiration for her boss.

For as long as she'd known Annabeth, the pretty red-headed baker had seemed like someone who had struck the jackpot in life—she had a wonderful and utterly devoted husband, a thriving business, healthy kids, and everyone in Bearpaw Ridge liked and respected her.

Annabeth nodded. "I was so scared that I was shaking by the time I loaded that last box in my car. Roger was at work, but I kept looking over my shoulder, thinking that he was going to come charging out of nowhere and smash my car to keep me from leaving. Maybe even smash me."

She shuddered visibly, her expression filled with remembered pain.

Then she looked up and smiled at Hannah. "And you know what? That sick feeling in my stomach from all those nerves—it vanished as soon as I'd made it safely over the Bay Bridge and merged onto Highway 80 heading east towards Sacramento and the mountains. That's when I knew that I'd made the right decision, and it didn't matter how angry Roger got, or how disappointed my mother was going to be when she realized that she wasn't getting the son-in-law of her dreams."

Annabeth understood, really and truly understood what Hannah going through right now. Hannah felt like crying with relief.

And she knew what she had to do. Even if it inconvenienced the people who counted on her to be here every day.

Even if it made her mom sad.

"I'm going to Australia." Her voice came out shaky, but she'd said it. She'd made the commitment.

Her decision made, Hannah felt the gray fog of loss and depression lifting. *Maybe it's not too late. Sam said that he'd wait for me... and he's been in touch every day since he left.*

Then that little voice that always tried to talk her out of taking chances spoke up again. *How do you know that you're not making a huge mistake?*

Annabeth said, "Good for you! And even if things don't work out in the end, at least you won't be sitting around in ten years, wondering what might have been." Her dimples came out in full force. "Though I'm really going to miss working with you. You've been my star employee and the glue that's held this place together through various crises. But I wish you all the happiness in the world, Hannah. You deserve it, and more."

Hannah took a deep breath. Now that she'd finally made the decision, she had a lot of things she needed to do to make her trip a reality.

But she felt alive again after all that terrible numbness and apathy. Excitement sang through veins, mixed with a bit of nervousness. It was a heady mixture.

"I don't suppose you'd let me work some overtime, so that I can save up for the plane ticket?"

Annabeth laughed, her eyes warm and sparkling. "Let me think about what I can do, and I'll get back to you." She leaned forward and put her hand over Hannah's. "We're going to make this happen for you, Hannah. You just needed to decide whether this is what you really wanted."

"I do want it. More than anything," Hannah said, fervently. "Sam was meant to be my mate, and I was meant to be his. I just let my fear get in the way."

Deep inside her, Hannah felt her bear stir awake at last.

～

After her shift at Cinnamon + Sugar finished, Hannah returned to the house that she shared with Kayla.

Kayla had put a beef stew in the slow-cooker for dinner, and the savory scents of browned meat, garlic, onions, and wine greeted Hannah when she stepped through the front door.

She fired up her laptop to check airfares and to check her bank account to find out how much money she needed to save before she could book her trip.

She was shocked to see a message from the bank, notifying about a large deposit recently made to her account.

Puzzled, she checked her balance, and saw that enough money to pay for an airline ticket to Australia had mysteriously appeared in her checking account.

Her phone buzzed with an incoming text.

It was from her mom.

My dear, Ash told me that he knows a passport expediting agency that can get you a passport in just a couple of days. Tourist visas are only $25, and once you book your ticket, the airline will take care of it for you if you scan in your passport and email it to them.

"I don't believe it," Hannah said out loud.

"What don't you believe?" Kayla asked, coming down the stairs.

She was dressed in a faded t-shirt and baggy sweats, and her hair was damp from a shower.

"I'm going to Australia, and I think Mom's on board with it." Hannah could hardly believe it.

Kayla whooped and took the remaining stairs in a single graceful leap, landing with a solid thump on the hardwood floor of the hall.

She hugged Hannah hard. "Took you long enough, Hannah-banana! I didn't want to say too much, but you were such a mess after Sam went home. When are you leaving? And how soon can I visit you there?"

"Are you that eager to get rid of me?" Hannah asked, laughing. "I don't know—I thought I was going to have work a bunch of extra shifts at the bakery—but now..." She shook her head. "I've got to phone Mom and thank her."

Giddy with excitement, she searched long minutes for her phone, then finally remembered it was in the back pocket of her jeans.

Kayla just stood there like the evil older sister that she was, and laughed at Hannah's discombobulation.

"Mom," she said when Margaret answered the call. "Thank you! Oh my God! I can't believe you did that!"

Margaret chuckled. "So, I'm guessing you found my little surprise?"

"Yes! But why? I thought you didn't want me to go!"

"Annabeth called me around lunchtime, and we had a nice long talk," her mother said.

Hannah remembered that her boss had excused herself to run an urgent errand just as the lunch rush was starting.

The realization that Annabeth had gone to bat for her made her want to cry with gratitude.

"And I realized I was wrong to try and hold you back," Margaret continued.

"It wasn't your fault," Hannah assured her. "I was scared and looking for a good excuse not to do the right thing."

"Your father would have wanted you to live life to the fullest," Margaret said. "And that's what I want for you, too. Go forth and have a grand adventure with your mate-to-be. I'll miss you like crazy, of course, but you need to live your life." She paused. "Just promise me that you'll come home for the holidays."

Hannah's eyes were overflowing with tears of joy. "No worries, Mom," she said, unconsciously echoing Sam's favorite phrase. "Sam's family does their Christmas in July. Now we'll have a reason to celebrate twice a year."

GOODBYE, HELLO

After a long, long flight that took her from Missoula through Salt Lake City and Los Angeles before the long stretch over the Pacific Ocean to Australia, Hannah's plane finally touched down in Brisbane.

She hadn't slept a wink in nearly two days of traveling because she had been so wound up with excitement and anticipation of seeing Sam again.

Her first impression of Queensland as they came in for their landing was of clear green ocean and dense suburbs, with lush vegetation that came right up to the edge of the coast. It looked nothing like the barren red rock desert that she'd been envisioning.

When she emerged from the Customs area of the airport, wearily dragging her suitcase behind her, the first thing she saw was a huge banner that read

Welcome To Oz, Hannah!

It was being held aloft by two grinning Australian firefighters that she recognized from their stint in Idaho.

And beneath the banner, holding a giant bouquet of Australian flowers—red and pink protea, banksia, and eucalyptus branches with silvery-green leaves—stood Sam, looking tall and tanned and impossibly handsome...and absolutely overjoyed to see her.

He strode forward as soon as he spotted her, and swept her up in his strong arms.

"God, I've missed you so much," he said, just before his mouth descended on hers in a long, deep kiss that made the very last of her doubts and fears vanish.

"I've missed you, too, you don't know how much. I'm so sorry it's taken me this long to make it here," she told him, when he let her up for breath.

"No worries," he said, glowing with happiness. "The only thing that matters is that you're here now. And you're even more beautiful than I remembered." Then he bent to give her another passionate kiss.

Her blood heated with desire and her heart pounded furiously.

She was dimly aware of his buddies whistling and clapping and cheering...joined by quite a few of the other people in the terminal.

But she didn't care. She had missed him so much, and she had been counting down the hours, minutes, seconds, until she could be in his arms again, like this, returning his kisses with same hunger that she sensed in him.

A long time later, but not nearly long enough, he finally drew back. "I'm so happy you've come to visit me. How long are you staying?"

Gazing deep into his bright blue eyes, Hannah reached up and touched his cheek, feeling the beloved, familiar stubble caress her fingertips. "As long as you want me to."

"How about forever?" he asked, slipping his arm around her shoulders and taking the handle of her suitcase from her. "Let me take you home, Hannah."

BOOKS BY OPHELIA SEXTON

Bearpaw Ridge Firefighters

- *Heat (Bearpaw Ridge Firefighters Book 1)*
- *Smolder (Bearpaw Ridge Firefighters Book 2)*
- *Ignite (Bearpaw Ridge Firefighters Book 3)*
- *Flame (Bearpaw Ridge Firefighters Book 4)*
- *Burn (Bearpaw Ridge Firefighters Book 5)*
- *Ash (Bearpaw Ridge Firefighters Book 6)*
- *Smoke (Bearpaw Ridge Firefighters Book 7)*
- *Blaze (Bearpaw Ridge Firefighters Book 8)*
- *Ember (Bearpaw Ridge Firefighters Book 9)*
- *Christmas in July (A Bearpaw Ridge Firefighters novella)*
- *Inferno (Bearpaw Ridge Firefighters Book 10)*
- *Scorch (Bearpaw Ridge Firefighters Book 11)*

Rocky Mountain Smokejumpers

- *Hard Landing (Rocky Mountain Smokejumpers Book 1)*
- *Jump Point (Rocky Mountain Smokejumpers Book 2)*

Beast Warriors (co-authored with Bliss Devlin)

- *Fugitive: A Werebear + BBW Paranormal Romance (Beast Warriors Book 1)* by Bliss Devlin and Ophelia Sexton
- *Hunter: A Werebear + BBW Paranormal Romance (Beast*

Warriors Book 2) by Bliss Devlin and Ophelia Sexton

- *Leader: A Werebear + Dragon Shifter Paranormal Romance (Beast Warriors Book 3)* – coming soon!

Made in the USA
Monee, IL
19 June 2021

71723378R00062